Published by Hachette Partworks Ltd
ISBN: 978-1-906965-44-0
Date of Printing: October 2010
Printed in Singapore by Tien Wah Press

# TinkerBell
### AND THE
## GREAT FAIRY RESCUE

## DISNEP
## Hachette

Tinker Bell and her fairy friends from Pixie Hollow were on their way to bring summer to the mainland – and Tink couldn't wait to get there!

Unlike the other seasons, summer needed the fairies' constant attention – which meant that Tink was going to be on the mainland for months instead of days.

Tinker Bell was so excited! She had heard that the fairy camp where they'd be staying was an amazing place.

Tink couldn't wait to
start tinkering!
"How's the beeliner workin'?"
she asked the animal fairies.
"Like a dream, Tink! Thanks!" they replied.
Tinker Bell couldn't find anything that
needed to be fixed, so she decided to look for
lost things.
Vidia couldn't believe that Tink wanted
to get CLOSER to the humans.

Suddenly, a loud *BANG!* echoed
through the camp, startling Fawn, who
splattered paint over the wing of a butterfly
she was painting. The other fairies hid under
leaves or between flowers.

Curious about the noise, Tinker Bell flew up
to get a better view, and spotted a car
driving down a winding road. Fascinated,
she chased after it.

Tinker Bell followed the car until it stopped at a country house. She hid and watched as a little girl named Lizzy got out with her father, Dr. Griffiths, and their cat, Mr. Twitches.

"Could we have a tea party in the meadow?" Lizzy pleaded as her father unloaded the suitcases.

"Not today," said Dr. Griffiths. "I have quite a bit of work to do. Perhaps tomorrow."

Tink waited until the humans were in the house, then flew down to examine the car. When Vidia found her, Tinker Bell was studying the engine.

"This is amazing!" Tink said. "Those wheels back there move because this chain thing rotates..."

"You shouldn't be this close to the human house!" Vidia interrupted.

But Tinker Bell had already darted inside the engine. She found an interesting-looking lever and turned it over and over again. Outside the car, each turn of the lever showered Vidia with water!

Just then, Lizzy and her father came back to unload the car. Lizzy spotted the butterfly – the one that had been splashed with paint.

"The wings have two entirely different patterns," Dr. Griffiths observed.

"Well, I guess that's just the way the fairies decided to paint it," Lizzy said.

"Lizzy, fairies are not real," Dr. Griffiths replied sternly.

But Lizzy really believed in fairies - so much so that she even had a little house for them to live in!

Tinker Bell and Vidia were ready to go back to fairy camp. But Vidia couldn't fly because her wings were still wet. Tink offered to walk with her.

Then Tink spotted a trail of buttons. "Wow! These will be perfect for the new wagon prototype I've been working on," she said. Then she realised that the buttons led right to Lizzy's fairy house!

"Tinker Bell, we're not supposed to go near human houses!" said Vidia.

"Come on, Vidia," said Tink. "It's perfectly safe."

Vidia wanted to teach Tink a lesson. She whipped up a gust of wind, which slammed the door shut.

Tink didn't mind. She was having fun exploring the miniature house's gadgets.

Suddenly, Vidia saw a human approaching. She pulled on the door to let Tink out, but it was jammed shut!

Vidia hid, watching fearfully as Lizzy peered into the house.

"A... a... a fairy!" Lizzy whispered in amazement.

She picked up the fairy house with Tinker Bell inside, and ran home! Lizzy put Tink in a cage to keep her safe from Mr. Twitches.

Vidia had to free Tink, but she knew she couldn't do it alone. She flew back to camp as fast as she could, but a sudden rainstorm slowed her down.

Vidia arrived back at the camp and told the other fairies what had happened.

They couldn't fly to Tink's rescue, because the storm was still raging. So Clank and Bobble built a boat to get them there.

But on the way, the boat ran aground at the foot of a waterfall and the fairies had to travel the rest of the way on foot. What a journey!

Back at the country house, Lizzy let Tinker Bell out of the cage.

Tinker Bell was amazed by Lizzy's fairy collection. But the little girl had her fairy facts all wrong! Tink tried to tell Lizzy, but all Lizzy heard was a jingling sound.

"So that's how fairies speak!" she exclaimed.

Tinker Bell wanted to tell Lizzy all about fairy life. So Lizzy asked questions, and Tink acted out her answers.

Lizzy decided to put all her fairy research down in the journal her father had given her. Soon, the journal was filled with drawings of Tink's fairy friends and descriptions of their special talents.

When Lizzy's Fairy Field Journal was complete, it was time for Tink to go and find her friends. Tinker Bell was sad about leaving Lizzy, but excited to go home.

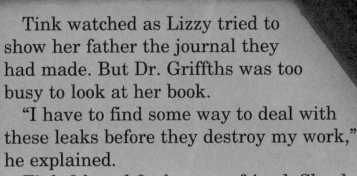

Tink watched as Lizzy tried to
show her father the journal they
had made. But Dr. Griffths was too
busy to look at her book.

"I have to find some way to deal with
these leaks before they destroy my work,"
he explained.

Tink felt sad for her new friend. She decided
to stay a while longer and help.

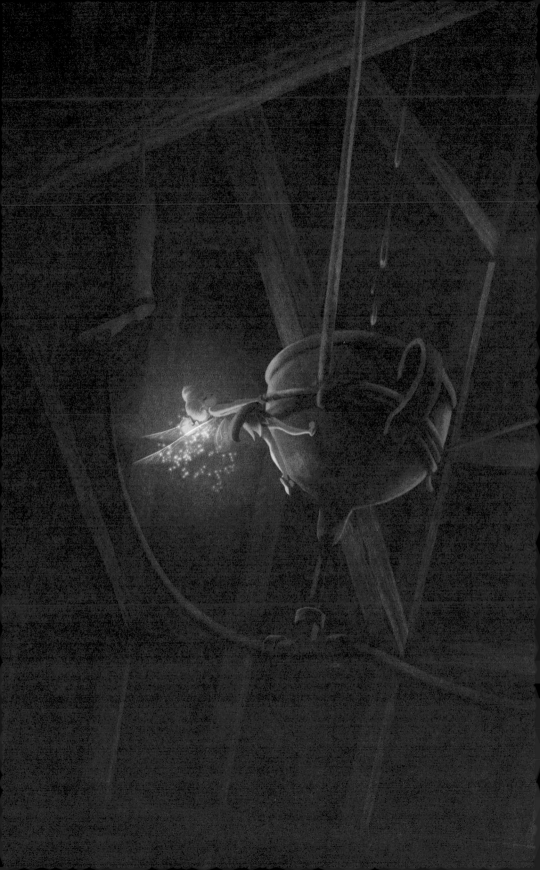

Tinker Bell had a plan. If she could help Dr. Griffiths with the house repairs, he would have more time to spend with Lizzy. Tink rummaged through the attic until she had all the parts she needed. In no time, she rigged up a system to take the water from the leaks and funnel it all back outside again.

As Tink flew back to Lizzy's room, she passed by Dr. Griffiths' study. She spotted the butterfly trapped in a jar.

Tinker Bell wanted to help the butterfly, so she opened the jar and set it free.

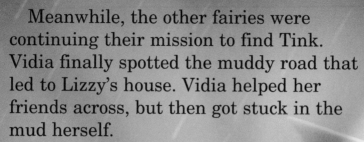

Meanwhile, the other fairies were continuing their mission to find Tink. Vidia finally spotted the muddy road that led to Lizzy's house. Vidia helped her friends across, but then got stuck in the mud herself.

Suddenly, they saw the headlights of a vehicle coming towards them!

"Pull! Pull!" cried Rosetta desperately – but Vidia was stuck fast in the mud.

Iridessa knew what she had to do. She bounced
the headlight beams back toward the driver, who
instantly slammed on his brakes.

Moments later, the driver got out of his car.
Fawn noticed that the driver's shoelace was
untied. "Grab this!" she told the other fairies.

They all held on to the shoelace. As the driver
turned to get back in his car, they were pulled out
of the mud!

In the morning, Dr. Griffiths discovered that the leaks seemed to have mended themselves! But he also noticed that the butterfly was gone, and sent Lizzy to her room. To cheer her up, Tink showered Lizzy with pixie dust. It was time for some flying lessons!

Downstairs, the fairy rescue team had finally arrived. They had to get to Tink, but Mr. Twitches had other ideas! The other fairies fought the cat off, while Vidia bounded up the stairs.

Meanwhile, Dr. Griffiths stormed into Lizzy's room.

"What's going on in here?" he demanded.

"I was flying. My fairy showed me how," explained Lizzy.

But Dr. Griffiths didn't believe her.

Tinker Bell had had enough. She flew out, straight into the face of Dr. Griffiths!

Dr. Griffiths tried to catch Tinker Bell in a jar. But poor Vidia, trying to help Tink, was the one who ended up captured!

Dr. Griffiths couldn't wait to show his colleagues the fairy. He drove off to the city with Vidia.

How could the fairies save their friend? It was still raining, so they couldn't fly. Then Tink had an idea. She sprinkled pixie dust over Lizzy.

"All aboard!" cried Tinker Bell, as the fairies climbed into Lizzy's pockets.

Soon they caught up with the car. Dr. Griffiths saw Lizzy... and she was flying!

At last, Dr. Griffiths understood. Some things were not meant to be seen, just believed. He set Vidia free.

The next day, father and daughter finally had their tea party in the meadow – and it was a huge success!

"Tink, you found something to fix, after all," said Terence, as the fairies saw how happy Lizzy was.

"I guess I did!" Tink replied with a smile.